MJV   B&T   12-01-07 $15.95

KNUCKLEBOOM LOADERS LOAD LOGS

A TRIP TO THE SAWMILL

Vermont forest as seen from the Goodridge Sawmill.

KNUCKLEBOOM LOADERS LOAD LOGS

A TRIP TO THE SAWMILL

Joyce Slayton Mitchell
photographs by Steven Borns

THE OVERLOOK PRESS
Woodstock & New York

Dedication

For Ethan Slayton and Audrey Dix Malila,

third cousins and Vermonters

who are growing up to love

and protect the Green Mountains.

—JSM

Sources and Acknowledgments

It is a pleasure to thank Colleen Goodridge, sawmiller, and Ken Davis, logger, who provided everything we needed to know and see in order to write and photograph this book. Time, conversations, trade magazines, field trips, more time, as well as introductions to other sawmillers, loggers, state foresters, saw doctor, landowners, truck drivers, knuckleboom loader loggers, feller buncher logger, and the sawdust man were all part of our education.

Colleen Goodridge of Goodridge Lumber, Inc. in Albany, Vermont and her sawyer sons Douglas, Mark, and Brian are eager for us all to know how sawmillers and loggers conserve our forests, America's only renewable natural resource. The Goodridge mission is to recycle every single fiber of each log brought into the sawmill: the bark, slabs, edges, short ends, chips, and sawdust, as well as sawn logs and lumber all leave the sawmill in a reusable form.

Ken Davis of Davis Contracting Service, Professional Timber Harvesting, in Hardwick, Vermont loves the woods. He knows that cutting trees is good for the forests and he is quick to point out that a well-managed forest has to be thinned in order to keep our woods strong. I am especially grateful to Ken for his time, thoughts, and expertise in logging which he so enthusiastically shared.

I am grateful, too, to Caledonia-Essex County Forester, Stephen Slayton, and Orleans County Forester, George Buzzell, for conversations, statistics, stories, and articles about Vermont and national forests, natural resources, and an understanding of the cooperation in Vermont between foresters, loggers, and sawmillers. Virginia Anderson, the Vermont Conservation Education Chief, has my thanks for her time, and the great variety of resources provided about forestry and environmental issues for children.

Special appreciation goes to Bruce Dexter, saw doctor of Sawmill Tool & Service Co., in Lyndonville, Vermont for the time he gave us to help us understand saw doctoring well enough for authentic photographs and text. We want to thank Kevin Barrup and his son Eric, of Green Mountain Mulch in Derby, Vermont, who gave us complete access to his family mulching plant. Thanks also goes to the tailers and graders of Goodridge Lumber: Dean Gonyaw, Michael Grondin, and Richard Mason; to feller buncher operator Willie McAllister; to Bob Stevens, general manager of Manosh Sawmill in Morrisville, Vermont; and to the sawdust man, Marc Delaricheliere.

Standing in the Goodridge Sawmill yard surrounded by the Green Mountains of Vermont, looking at the piles of logs and lumber, chips and sawdust; watching the knuckleboom loader load the logs, the fork loaders loading the log deck, the bucket loader filling the sawdust truck; and smelling the freshly cut cedar, this all comes together as a distinctive, unforgettable experience.

INTO THE WOODS

• • • • • • • • • • • • • • • • • • • •

The logger takes the 167-horsepower feller buncher and
the 174-horsepower skidder (with chains on its four tires),
out to the Vermont logging site. The county forester has
marked the best trees to cut in order to manage a healthy
forest. The unmarked trees are left to grow and reseed
themselves.

The feller buncher operator checking the cutting tooth.

The feller buncher grabs the tree . . .   . . . and shears it at its base.

The feller buncher shears the marked trees with a wide 2½ inch kerf cutting tooth, spinning at 200 miles per hour (mph). The kerf is the width of the cut made by the saw. The feller buncher can cut and hold 3 to 4 trees all at once before they are dropped in a pile for the skidder to move them out to the landing.

The feller buncher holding a tree.

A grapple skidder with chains on its tires for the best traction.

The logger unwraps the choker chain at the landing.

A cable skidder drags the log along the logging trail.

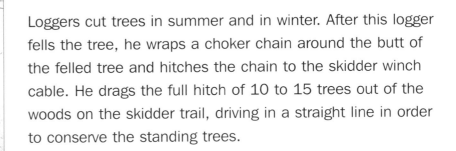

Loggers cut trees in summer and in winter. After this logger fells the tree, he wraps a choker chain around the butt of the felled tree and hitches the chain to the skidder winch cable. He drags the full hitch of 10 to 15 trees out of the woods on the skidder trail, driving in a straight line in order to conserve the standing trees.

The delimber scrapes limbs and leaves off the tree.

The slasher saw operator cuts logs to the longest length he can get.

ON THE LANDING

A 400-pound slasher saw whirling at 1,200 rpm's.

The landing is an area near the forest where 22-wheelers can pick up the logs. The skidder piles the trees beside the delimber, which cuts all of the leaves and limbs off the trees before they are cut and trucked. The slasher saw logger picks up each delimbed tree and figures out the longest log he can get out of it. Then he cuts the tree with his 400-pound slasher saw, which whirls around at 1,200 revolutions per minute (rpm). All of the tree top limbs, twigs, and leaves are fed into the chipper. The chips are sold to electrical plants to make electricity, to schools and businesses for heating fuel, and to paper mills to be made into thousands of kinds of paper products.

Delimbed and cut on the landing; ready for the logging truck.

A knuckleboom loader loads logs.

OFF THE LANDING

The logs are loaded onto the logging truck with a knuckleboom loader. The top-grade logs are trucked to sawmills and the lower-grade logs to paper mills.

Trucking off the landing.

An early morning logging truck arrives at the sawmill.

INTO THE SAWMILL

The tractor-trailer trucker drives his 22-wheeler into the sawmill where the white cedar logs are unloaded with a knuckleboom loader, then piled and scaled.

A knuckleboom loader unloads logs while logs are scaled below.

The first job in the sawmill is to measure, or scale, each log to find out how many board feet (bf) can be cut from each of them. The scaler measures the diameter of the small end of each log, inside the bark, and enters the number on the scaling sheet. The scaling sheet has a Vermont Log Rule table that indicates the volume of board feet for each log, using a quarter inch kerf. The first log measured here is 12 feet by 10 inches.

A 22-wheeler logging truck.

Scaling for board feet in the log.

VERMONT LOG RULE

	LOG LENGTH (feet)						
DIAMETER	**8'**	**9'**	**10'**	**11'**	**12'**	**13'**	**14'**
4 (inches)	5	6	7	7	8	9	9
5	8	9	10	11	13	14	15
6	12	14	15	17	18	20	21
7	16	18	20	22	25	27	29
8	21	24	27	29	32	35	37
9	27	30	34	37	41	44	47
10	33	38	42	46	50	54	58
11	40	45	50	55	61	66	71
12	48	54	60	66	72	78	84
13	56	63	70	77	85	92	99
14	65	74	82	90	98	106	114
15	75	84	94	103	113	122	131
16	85	96	107	117	128	139	149
17	96	108	120	132	145	157	169
18	108	122	135	149	162	176	189
19	120	135	150	165	181	196	211
20	133	150	167	183	200	217	233
21	147	165	184	202	221	239	257
22	161	182	202	222	242	262	282
23	176	198	220	242	265	287	309
24	192	216	240	264	288	312	336
25	208	234	260	286	313	339	365
26	225	254	282	310	338	366	394
27	243	273	304	334	365	395	425
28	261	294	327	359	392	425	457
29	280	315	350	385	421	456	491
30	300	338	375	413	450	488	525
31	320	360	400	440	481	521	561
32	341	384	427	469	512	555	597
33	363	408	454	499	545	590	635
34	385	434	482	530	578	626	674
35	408	459	510	561	613	664	715
36	432	486	540	594	648	702	756
37	456	513	570	627	685	742	799
38	481	542	602	662	722	782	842
39	507	570	634	697	761	824	887
40	533	600	667	733	800	867	933

Look at the intersection of the Vermont Log Rule table and you will see that this log will provide a volume of 50 board feet. The Vermont rule favors small and short logs because most of the Vermont trees are smaller than the trees in the Northwest. The International Log Rule predicts only 45 board feet for a tree 12 feet by 10 inches. Loggers use the rule that predicts the most board feet for their load of logs.

The fork lift carries logs from the yard . . .

. . . to the log deck of the sawmill.

White cedar in the mill yard.

Scaled white cedar logs ready for the log deck.

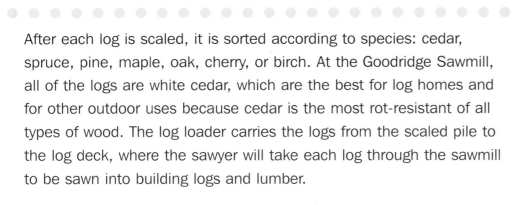

After each log is scaled, it is sorted according to species: cedar, spruce, pine, maple, oak, cherry, or birch. At the Goodridge Sawmill, all of the logs are white cedar, which are the best for log homes and for other outdoor uses because cedar is the most rot-resistant of all types of wood. The log loader carries the logs from the scaled pile to the log deck, where the sawyer will take each log through the sawmill to be sawn into building logs and lumber.

Open jaws of the cutter
head of the debarker.

A giant chain conveyor and roller
moves the log into the cutting knives.

The conveyor belt carries slabs to a chipper before they are blown into a truck.

Wood chips blown into a truck.

Inside the sawmill the log rolls down the deck onto rollers. The rollers feed the log into the cutter head of the debarker, where cutting knives remove the bark by moving around and around the length of the log. The bark drops off the deck onto a conveyer belt that carries it under the sawmill, where it will be blown into a truck that will take bark, slabs, and chips to a mulching plant.

Early morning fog lifts in the Green Mountain mulching yard, while a bucket loader dumps woodchips.

A bucket load of bark chips for the wood hog.

Bucket loader to wood hog.

Bark, slabs, and chips from the sawmills are sold to mulching plants which load them into the wood hog with their bucket loaders. At the mulch plant, the bark and chips are ground and dyed until they are the right size and color for gardening and landscaping.

Dyed and sized mulch ready to package.

Top, left: First cuts take off the slabs.

Left: The head saw squares the log.

Top, right: A tailer grabs the squared log from the head saw.

After being debarked, the log travels on the roller deck to the carriage which carries it to the 50-inch, 100-pound head saw. There, the first cuts will take off the round sides of the log until it is square. The rounded first cuts are called slabs. The slabs drop onto a vibrating conveyer belt where they are carried to the wood-chipper. The chipper cuts the slabs into small woodchips that are blown into a truck and taken to paper mills or mulching plants.

A first cut slab drops to the conveyer belt.

From head saw to double edger.

The laser beams show the sawyer where to cut.

The double edger cuts the board width.

After the slabs are cut, the cut boards are put through the double edger, where two 15-inch saws remove the wane—the rough edges at the ends of the boards. The board is measured by a laser beam in order to get the widest board possible out of the piece of timber. When the board rolls out of the double edger, a tailer picks it up, grades it for quality, and decides what length to cut it on his trim saw.

The trim saw drops down to cut the board length.

The tailer grabs the sawn, edged, and
trimmed board and carries it by hand out
of the mill to be dried.

The logs and lumber are dried by using stickers to separate the boards and let the air circulate through the lumber piles. Stickers are one to two inches wide, exactly one inch thick, and as long as the pile is wide. They are made from straight, dry lumber which is free from knots. This keeps the boards even as they dry. Stickers are placed perpendicular to the length of the boards, 12 to 18 inches apart.

As a saw whirls through a log, tiny pieces of wood fly through the air. These are sucked into a pipe and blown into the sawdust shed. A bucket loader picks up the sawdust from the shed and loads it into a truck. Sawdust is used for farm animal bedding, among other things.

A bucket load of sawdust . . . from the sawdust shed . . . is dumped into a farmer's truck.

In the sawmill the sawyer sometimes has to retooth the blade of the saw so that the saw can make a finer cut in the logs. He measures the kerf and sharpens the sawteeth, so that the saw will conserve more of the log and make less sawdust. When the circular saw gets bent, loses tension, or the shank that holds the teeth gets broken, the saw has to go to the saw doctor.

Opposite page:
Top, left: Replacing the shank.
Bottom: A new tooth in a new shank.
Top, right: Final task—sharpening the teeth.

This page:
Top: Measuring the tension with a straight edge.

Middle: Correcting the tension with the twistface hammer.

Bottom: The cross-peen finishes the job.

The saw doctor is sometimes called a hammerman because he fixes the saw by pounding it with an 8-, 6-, or 4-pound hammer. The hammers have different shapes in order to make exact corrections. Most of the time the hammerman uses the twistface or the doghead 8-pound hammers. Sometimes, he uses the cross-peen 6- or 8-pounder.

This planer has one tooth to cut a groove into the side of the log.

The planer smooths out the sawn lumber.

After the trimmed lumber has dried, it goes to the planer where it is smoothed and grooved. The best white cedar logs in the millyard will be used for top-grade building logs and lumber. The secondary white cedar is sawn into lumber that will be used for building barns, decks, and fences.

Measuring the planed log with a straight edge.

Feeding the planer.

The tailer stacks the dried
and planed boards.

The resaw shed: getting the
most out of imperfect logs.

An extra band saw sits on top of
the logs just in case . . .

Cants, the squared logs that have had their rounded ends
removed by the head saw, are ready for the resaw. The resaw
gets the best use out of every log by using a band saw with a
3/32-inch kerf, which makes a very thin cut through the cant.

A very thin cut through the
cant with the band saw.

Tightening the straps—
ready to roll.

Leaving the Vermont millyard
wih a full load of hard maple.

OUT WITH THE SAWN LUMBER

The sawn dried logs and lumber are loaded on to a flat bed
with a log loader . . . ready to build. This 18-wheeler is loaded
with 8,513 board feet of hard maple to be trucked to a pallet
plant. The red Goodridge truck is loaded with sawn logs ready
to be put together for a new log home.

Grooved logs for a new home.

IN WITH THE LOGS

The log-truck trucker delivers a load of white cedar logs . . . ready to mill.

The knuckleboom loader unloads logs.

Timber Talk and Glosary

Air-drying: Seasoning lumber in the open air, using spacers to separate the boards.

Band saw: An endless belt-like blade of steel, toothed on one or both edges, used to saw lumber.

Bit: A tooth for a circular saw.

Board foot (bf): A unit of measure.

Board side: The side of a saw that the board passes while being cut.

Cant: A squared log that has been slabbed on each side, ready for the resaw.

Cant hook: A 5-7-foot lever, fitted at the end with a ring used to move the slabbed logs.

Carriage: The frame on which a log is held, it moves forward and back while the log is sawn.

Chips: The parts of wood, scrap pieces, strips or edges that are recycled when logs are sawn.

Choker chain: Slips tight over logs as the skidder pulls the load.

Circular Saw: A circular plate with cutting teeth on the circumference and used to rip-saw logs.

Conveyor chain: An endless chain used for carrying material from place to place.

Cord: A pile of wood 4 feet high, 4 feet wide, and 8 feet long.

Cruise: To go through the forest measuring timber.

Deck: The platform in a sawmill on which logs are collected and stored before they are placed on the carriage for sawing.

Deckman: The person who aligns logs on the deck and rolls them down for loading on the carriage.

Dimensional lumber: Yard lumber that measures from two to five inches thick and any width.

Dog: A steel tooth that is attached to the carriage and operated by a lever. Carriage dogs are used to hold the log firmly on the carriage.

Dog board: The last board in the log to which the carriage dogs are attached.

Dogging: Fixing and releasing the dogs in the log or board.

Dog housing: The metal frame supporting the dog.

Dressed lumber: Lumber that was been trimmed and planed on one or both sides.

Edge: To make square-edged.

Edgings: Strips cut from the edges of logs for the chipper.

Edger: A machine with two saws used to remove wane from sawn boards and to rip lumber into narrower pieces.

Even-aged: A stand or forest that consists of trees that are within ten to twenty years of one another.

Feller buncher: a machine that cuts a tree with a shear and carries one or more cut trees in its hydraulically operated arms as it moves to cut the next tree.

Filer: A person who sharpens saws in a sawmill.

Gig: Running the sawmill carriage back after a board is cut from the log.

Grader: The one who stands with the tailer and grades each board off the saw.

Green: Unseasoned lumber, wet.

Gullet: The rounded cavity on a saw where sawdust accumulates and is carried from the cut.

Hammering: The science of tensioning and leveling a saw blade.

Hammerman: Saw doctor or sawsmith - one who fixes saws.

Hot Yard: Logging site where cutting is taking place.

Kerf: The width of a cut made by a saw.

Knuckleboom loader: A machine that swings to load, with a grapple and a supporting structure designed to pick up and discharge trees for piling, loading, and unloading logs.

Landing: An area in or near the forest where cut logs are delimbed, sawed into log lengths and loaded for transport out of the woods.

Log dog: A metal bracket attached at intervals to the log-haul chain to prevent slippage in logs being transported from the yard to the sawmill.

Log rule: A table showing the estimated number of board feet (bf) of lumber that can be sawed from logs of various lengths and diameters.

Log scale: The board feet (bf) content of logs as determined by a log rule.

Lumber boards: Lumber less than two inches thick, 8 inches or more in width.

Miles Per Hour (mph): A measuring unit.

Pallet: A wooden, four-foot square platform used to store and transport goods by forklift, 18-wheelers, air and sea.

Renewable resource: a naturally occurring resource, such as trees, that is continually replenished through biological growth and reproduction.

Resaw: A bandsaw with a fine cut used to reduce cants to a useable product.

Revolutions per minute (rpm): A means of measuring saw speed.

Saw doctor: Hammerman or sawsmith—one who fixes saws.

Scale: To measure logs for board feet (bf).

Saw kerf: The width of a cut made by a saw.

Sawyer: The person who runs the head saw in a sawmill.

SFPM: Surface Feet Per Minute, a means of measuring saw speed.

Shank: The piece of metal that holds the saw tooth in place and creates the gullet on the circular saw.

Skid: To drag trees or logs to the landing area.

Slab: The outside portion of a log that is removed to get a flat face for sawing lumber.

Slash: The stumps, limbs, twigs, and wood chunks left after trees have been felled.

Slasher saw: The 400-pound circular saw mounted on the log-loader used to cut logs into lengths suitable for the sawmill or paper mills.

Sticker: A piece of lumber that separates the different boards in a pile in order to air dry the lumber.

Tailer: The one who stands directly behind the headsaw in the mill and grabs slabs and boards as they come off the saw, placing them flat on the rollers to the chipper or edger.

Trim saw: A circular, drop saw that cuts overlength of board.

Timber: A felled tree at least five inches at the smallest end.

Wane: Bark or the rough edges on the corners of a board.

Yard lumber: Lumber that is less than 5 inches thick used in general building.

Forest Facts

- The tallest redwood ever measured was 367 feet tall. That's 62 feet taller than the Statue of Liberty.

- Albizzia trees of Malaysia are among the fastest growing trees in the world. Some can grow as much as 30 feet in one year - that's almost an inch a day.

- Each American uses the equivalent of a 100-foot tree each year.

- Americans need over 600 pounds of paper a year for books, diapers, packaging and all other paper products they use.

- A 12-year old child needs to plant and maintain 65 trees in order to offset the amount of carbon that child will put in the atmosphere during the rest of his or her lifetime.

- Each person needs 365 pounds of oxygen to breathe each year - and most of that oxygen is manufactured by growing trees.

- An acre of trees can remove about 13 tons of dust and gases every year from the surrounding environment.

- When trees stop growing, they start to use oxygen, rather than produce it for us to breathe.

- America has 70% of the forestland that was here in 1600 - there are 737 million acres of forest in the U.S.

- Over 1.5 billion trees are planted in the U.S. - more than 5 trees for every man, woman and child in America. That averages 4.1 million seedlings each day.

- Each year, six trees are planted for every one that is cut.

Web Sites

For kids:
www.realtrees4kids.org
www.talkabouttrees.org
www.foresters.org/kidz

For teachers:
Project Learning Tree, a K-12 curriculum, Vermont Conservation Education:
www.plt.org

First published in the United States in 2003 by
The Overlook Press, Peter Mayer Publishers, Inc.
Woodstock & New York

WOODSTOCK:
One Overlook Drive
Woodstock, NY 12498
www.overlookpress.com
[For individual orders, bulk and special sales, contact our
Woodstock office]

NEW YORK:
141 Wooster Street
New York, NY 10012

Text copyright © 2003 Joyce Slayton Mitchell
Photographs © 2003 Steven Borns

A CIP record for this book is available from the Library of
Congress

Book design and type formatting by Bernard Schleifer

Printed in Singapore

ISBN 1-58567-368-4
9 8 7 6 5 4 3 2 1